THE UNNERVING

BY

M.A. SAVINO

Contents

Chapter One-Noise

The silence in our house provided little serenity for my chattering mind. I tried reading to think of anything else but Jamie, but it didn't work. I couldn't concentrate on the words enough to decipher their meaning. His sudden disappearance had the entire town on edge. I feared that breaking up with him might have something to do with it, but I hoped not.

We had only dated for a couple of weeks when he breached my body with his, taking away my title as the only virgin in senior high. Although he graduated, he still came to school daily to pick up his friends so they could run the streets. That is how we met. He threw a party by the train tracks, and everyone showed up.

I lied to my parents that night and told them I would stay with my friend, and she did the same.

When I laid eyes on him, I knew I wanted him to be my first. After that night, we were inseparable, and our relationship became the talk of the entire school. I am the valedictorian, and dating the bad boy made for an endless supply of gossip.

There was nothing I wouldn't do for Jamie's attention. My best friend, Lisa, tried to tell me that it was because my father never paid my sister and me any mind. He used to when we were little, but it had become less over the years. His affection nowadays consisted of a hug if we were sad and a few words of greeting or farewell at the beginning or end of the day.

When my mom found out about Jamie and me, she shut the relationship down at once and made me leave him. I never told her we had sex, but her suspicions multiplied when he refused to stay away.

The last time he came to my house, he tossed stones at my glass to get my attention. His baby face and attentive ways were irresistible to my inexperienced heart.

I wanted him back, and tried to sneak away so we could talk, but my mother caught me climbing out of my window.

She snatched me by the seat of my pants, pulled me back into my room, and nailed it shut. His persistent phone calls and late-night visits were wearing on her.

My father ignored the situation by napping in his favorite chair, but my mother was another story. It got to the point where she just took the telephone off the hook and stopped answering the door when he came.

One day, I received a letter from him through a mutual friend. The burned cigarette holes penetrated through every place he had written the word 'love,' so there were many openings.

I held it and cried alone in the school bathroom stall. I didn't want this to happen, for I loved him too, but if we stayed together, I couldn't hang out with any of my friends. All their parents agreed with my mother on a united front, making my decision agonizing. No more friends, and go against her wishes or lose the boyfriend. I chose the latter. As I read his note, I feared I had made the wrong decision.

"Anna, are you in here?" Lisa's voice echoed against the walls of the girl's tiled bathroom.
"Yes."
"You, okay?"
"No," I said, pushing the stall door open.

I handed her the textured message without saying a word. Lisa's hand shook as she ran her fingers over the textured rings of singed paper.

"Anna, maybe you should tell your parents."
"No. You don't understand. I love him."
"I know, but he's escalating, and I don't want something bad to happen," Lisa said, concerned.
"Please don't say anything."
"I won't, but I'm worried."

We walked together that day. I usually walk alone, but Lisa insisted. The freshly paved road home smelled like asphalt and welcomed our bare feet. Indian summer improved my mood, so I planned to enjoy it. The impending winters of New York could be treacherous and were always so depressing.
Days after Jamie's friend had passed me the punctured letter, rumors of his disappearance began. I thought he had given up on us, but that wasn't the case. As it turned out, the rumors were true—his uncle, whom he lived with, filed a missing person report with the police department. No one had seen Jamie for a week, and the news of his vanishing hit

me hard. I feel partly to blame, and my parents were less supportive of my feelings.

Because our town is so tiny, you couldn't go anywhere without someone bringing up their theories and assumptions about where he was or what had happened.

When Thanksgiving break came, my mother thought it would be best to get away for a while, so we escaped to our sizeable mountainside getaway. They planned to sell it in the spring, but they had been saying that for years. It was my father's childhood home, and he had a difficult time letting go.

Whistles of wind pierced through the aged, rattling windows as snow blanketed the earth. Although the weather outside was disappointing, the fluffy white flakes appeared so beautiful on the trees and surrounding landscaping.

A glass-tapping twig from the nearby maple tree became increasingly annoying, so I slipped my father's boots on and went to address it.

The blustery snow stung my face and impaired my vision as I snapped off the branch and threw it on the ground. When I came back inside, my mother was waiting for me with her hands on her hips.

"Anna, what the heck are you doing? And where is your darn coat?"

"Sorry, mom. A twig was hitting the glass, so I broke it off."

"Well, wear a jacket next time."

"Yes, ma'am."

She walked out of the room, and I went back to reading. The tapping returned like a taunting little sister, but Emma was asleep, and only two, so it couldn't have been her.

I threw my book in frustration, pulled my father's boots back on with a jacket this time, and went back outside. The piece of wood, now partially covered in snow, still lay where I had left it. No other tree branches were close to the glass.

When I turned toward the vast landscape behind me, a dark shadowy figure manifested before me. My body flailed backward, struck the unforgiving ground, and my teeth clamped down onto my tongue.

I spit the blood from my mouth as the metallic liquid coated the inside, nauseating me. A loud knocking on the transparent barrier above my head spooked me. My mother's hand waved at me through the frosty glass to come in. I refocused my sights from her back to the yard, but nothing was there. My mind was playing tricks on me; I slapped my cold palms into the white fluff, stood up, and yelled at myself in frustration.

"You're losing it, Anna!"

A thick squall made it even more challenging to see. My freezing fingers burned as I brushed my butt off and hustled back into the house. My parents were sitting on the sofa blankly when I came in.

"What?"
"Anna, you need to come to sit down. We have something to tell you."

My face froze as they ripped my heart out with the news. The police found Jamie's body in the woods close to our house in town. They continued to tell me what they knew, but I couldn't hear them. My stomach and head felt like a twisted mess of heartache and despair.

"Anna, I'm so sorry," my mother said, with tears streaking her makeup.
"Mom, what happened?"
"They haven't released a cause of death yet."
"Is it because of me?" I said, sobbing.
"Of course not, sweetheart."
"I want to go home."
"We are going back in the morning. For right now, Anna, you get some rest," she said, patting me on the thigh.

Rest. What is rest? How can I sleep when my love is dead, and it is my fault? I'm sure my parents were relieved that he was gone. My swollen eyes burned from crying, but I couldn't turn off the faucet.
The memory of his face and touch will be etched in my mind for eternity. The way he used to hold me and gaze into my eyes would give me butterflies that, even now, I can feel.
I should have given everything up for him, but I was too afraid. My path had been strategically laid out for me for years. According to my parents, school, college, career, husband, and family were the keys to

my success, but that was their dream for me, not mine. I wanted something else. I wanted love, but it is too late for that now.

My head sunk into my pillow, and tears went from my eyes, down my cheeks, and into my ears. I didn't bother wiping them away. What would be the point? My eyes grew heavy with exhaustion, and sleep came without trying.

The feel of my blanket sliding off me took me out of unconsciousness. I jumped out of bed and turned on the light. My sister Emma stood in the doorway of my room, giggling.

"Emma?"
"Hi, sissy."
"Hi. Find mommy and go away."
"Okay."

She took off yelling. The sound of her pattering feet slapped the old wood as she went. This house was the last place I wanted to be, and I couldn't wait to go home. The dark red Victorian wallpaper felt gloomy and made me feel more depressed.

My father just came out of the only bathroom in the house and brought the fumes from his toilet time with him.

"Jeepers, dad," I said, holding my nose.
"Sorry, it must have been the chicken and broccoli from the other night."
"You could have at least sprayed," I said, waving my hand in the air.
"Well, Anna, I would have, but we are out."

He continued to his bedroom and vanished, leaving me in front of the gas chamber. I plugged my nostrils and went in to do my business.

The claw tub next to me held a bunch of toys from Emma's bath the night before. A round plastic one with a toy inside rested by my ankle.

I kicked it away from me, and it bounced off the old wall vent and headed back to me. It started fast, then stopped suddenly, like someone put their foot on it to stop it. Then it began rolling on its own towards the door.

I wiped, flushed the toilet, and bolted out of the bathroom. I wouldn't say I like this house with its old creepy vibes and age-stained wallpaper, but I appreciated its space.

When I went downstairs, breakfast sat idly at the table, waiting to be eaten. My parents whispered in the other room, and Emma gawked at me from her highchair.

"Hungry, Emma?"

She nodded her head aggressively, and I smiled. As annoying as she could be, I wouldn't let her starve because of my parent's inattentiveness. I cut her toast into small pieces and gave them to her. Then, I loaded eggs on her tray like a lunch lady.

She grabbed a stack of scrambled and shoved them in her mouth.

My plate was the same as hers, but I had bacon too. The salty crunch gratified my palette as I ate and continued reading.

Without warning, eggs smacked me in the face, followed by Emma laughing hysterically. She could be such a shit sometimes.

"Knock it off, Emma," my mother scoffed, entering the room.

She retrieved the pieces of egg off the floor and threw them in the garbage. I snatched a napkin and wiped the mush off my face while my father came and took a seat next to me.

"How are you doing, kiddo?"
"I'm okay."

He sat beside me, silent as though he was waiting for something to happen. I didn't like how unsettled the air became, so I turned to my mother.

"What?"

My mother pulled up a chair and sat down. Her shaking hand on my knee brought tears to my eyes. Whatever she was about to say would be bad; my mother doesn't get rattled, not by anything.

"We have something to tell you, and it's going to be upsetting. I want you to know that we are here for you no matter what you think." Her voice quivered as a tear tugged at the corner of her right eye.
"What is it? What news? Is it Jamie?"
"Yes," my father said.
"What, mom?"
"Sweetheart, Jamie was murdered."

The words caught in her throat and took me by surprise. My head started to spin, and dizziness would have taken me to the floor if it weren't for my father.

"What? Who did this? How? Was he stabbed? Shot? Why would someone do this?"

"I don't know, but the police are investigating, so I'm sure we will know more soon."

"It's my fault. Jamie would still be alive if I had just stayed with him."

"Sweetheart, don't say that," my father said, placing his hand on mine, then returned to eating.

"When is the funeral?"

"In… a few… days," my mother said in a choppy voice.

"Can I go?"

"Of course, we will take you."

My mother said 'we' as if my father had no say. When he became more withdrawn from my sister and me, I imagine he did the same with our mother. She always seemed tired and lonely. When she glanced at our father, you could see the disappointment in his lack of caring.

After breakfast, we packed our bags and left for town. The drive down the mountain always concerned me. Its winding roads and sharp, slippery turns made me afraid we would slide off the edge and crash.

My death grip on the seat would bend my soft nails backward and make marks in the upholstery. We were an hour away from home when my mother had to stop and use the restroom. My parents didn't want

to wake Emma, so I stayed in the car while they
went.

Christmas music played quietly on the radio, and
the windows fogged from our warm breath. When
they finally returned, we could barely see through the
windshield.

I leaned my head against the window, drew a sad
face with my finger, and sighed. My mother turned to
me and peered at the drawing.

"Anna, you're going to be fine."

Her words gave me no solace, for I am not okay,
and I don't think I will be ever again.

They say time heals all wounds, but that won't be the case for me. My broken heart sits in pieces at the base of my first true love's casket—his life taken away by some unknown stranger for a reason that has yet to be revealed.

My overloaded schedule filled with honors academic club sessions and classroom president meetings consumed a great deal of time. If do-overs were allowed, I would have given everything up for him and made more time, but it's too late now.

A vast crowd of gossiping teenagers and curious onlookers came to his funeral, hoping to get answers to the questions on their minds. The haughty popular girls of the senior class gawked at me from across the room. Their persistent whispers earned them several requests to be quiet from the adults around them. Lisa came to my side and took my hand.

"Don't let them get to you. They are just trying to get a reaction out of you," she said as she squeezed my palm.

"It's not right. They shouldn't even be here," I said while giving them an angry look.

"I know."

We listened as the pastor spoke about Jamie's life as if he knew him, but he didn't. Though our relationship only lasted a short time, we became close. He told me things about his family that few people knew. We shared many secrets that neither one of us would ever reveal. I, too, would take them to the grave just like he took mine with him.

After the viewing at the funeral home, we drove with the procession to the cemetery for his burial. The weather outside turned dismal with cold, wet misting rain.

Our heeled feet sank into the moist soil as we moved to the edge of Jamie's plot. One of the girls from the popular crowd lost her heel in the mud, and her bare foot went into a puddle.

I giggled at the sight of her disgusted face pulling the muddy shoe out of the ground. She shook the muck from it and shot me an evil glance.

Once the pastor gave his last sermon, people stopped at the casket for one final goodbye. Some of the crowd left flowers, and others left letters and pictures of themselves with Jamie. I had only one photo of us, and a single red rose to place on his mahogany enclosure.

Lisa had taken our picture a week before he and I broke up. We were locked in a staring contest trying not to laugh, but in the end, we began laughing simultaneously. The moment, captured by Lisa, showed our undeniable love for each other. My mother came over to me and rested her hand on my shoulder.

"Anna, it's time to go."
"Just a few more minutes, please, mom."
"Okay."

She walked away and stood with my father, so I could be alone. I put my hand on Jamie's death box and said goodbye.

"I'm so sorry I left you. It was the biggest mistake of my life. I wish I had stayed; this would never have happened. I love you."

"Anna?" An unfamiliar voice said.

"Yes?"

A man in a suit extended his hand to me as I looked around for my parents, but they were busy talking to neighbors. The man pulled his blazer aside, revealing a shiny gold badge.

"My name is detective Perez, and I wanted to know if I could ask you a few questions."

"About what?"

"Your relationship with the deceased," he said.

"I guess."

"Okay. Do you know anyone who wanted to hurt Jamie?"

"No."

"When was the last time you saw him?"

When I opened my mouth to answer, my mother intervened.

"Excuse me. Are you questioning our daughter without the presence of her parents?"

"Ma'am, it's just some standard questions."

"I don't care what it is. Now is not the time or the place to talk to her about anything. She's grieving the death of her boyfriend, and you have the nerve to grill her about it," she said, turning me away.

"Sorry. I meant no disrespect."

She took me by the arm and led me away from him—what a strange comment to make to the detective. The last thing she ever wanted was for Jamie to be with me, and now that he's gone, she addresses him as if we were together. Could it be that she felt guilty about forcing us to break up? I didn't have much to say to her or anyone else, for that matter, after the funeral.

I stayed in my room for the rest of the evening, thinking about my time with Jamie. We will meet again someday when I, too, have passed on. But for now, I will lie here on my tear-soaked pillow until my grief puts me into a deep slumber.

Shattering glass woke the whole house around midnight. My father ordered us to remain in our rooms as he moved toward the family room with his handgun.

This is the first time I have seen him so alert and focused in a long time. My hands shook as I listened to the darkness waiting for word from my father.

"All clear," he hollered.

I crept across the floor and met my mother, who carried Emma on her hip. When we entered the room, broken glass littered the carpet below the front window.

"Stay back," he said, holding his hand up.
"What is it, dad?"
"A crow hit the window."
"A crow? I thought they only flew during the day?"

He wrapped up the unmoving bird in a worn-out towel.

"Is it dead?" I asked.
"It is. I'm going to go take it outside."

My mother handed me Emma to help him clean up the mess. She picked up the large shards first and put them in the trash. Then she snatched the vacuum and went over the rug while my father brought in cardboard and tape to temporarily seal the hole.

I took Emma back to her room and tucked her into bed. She clenched my arm and pulled me to her for a hug. Even though she could be a spoiled brat, sometimes, she can be so sweet out of nowhere.

I tried to go back to sleep, but my mind wouldn't shut down. It scrambled with theories of who could have killed Jamie and why. He could be quite the troublemaker, but not so much that someone would want to kill him.

The creaking sound of my door opening distracted me from my thoughts. It stopped when I glimpsed at it.

"Emma, is that you?"

I didn't want to get out of bed, and she didn't answer, so I didn't bother. I closed my eyes and covered my tired head with a pillow.

My door stood ajar when I peeled my eyes open in the morning. I climbed out from under the covers and headed to the toilet. A few seconds after entering, there was a knock at the door.

"Anna, are you in there?"

"Yes, dad."

"Okay. I'm running to the store to get a new window, and your mom took Emma grocery shopping."

"All right."

I finished my business and went back to my room. It didn't feel like a Saturday, and I didn't want to get dressed. If I could stay in my pajamas until school on Monday, I would, but my parents would object for sure. My closet, overly filled with clothes I didn't even wear anymore, begged to be cleaned, so I started on the top shelf.

When I went to grab a box, the whispering sound of my name came from behind me.

"Annnnnnnaaaaaa."

I dropped the box and shouted.

"Jeepers, dad, you scared the crap out of me."

When I turned to face him, there was no one there. I peered around the room and on the back side of the closet door, but there was no one. I yelled louder.

"Dad?"

No answer. I left my room and searched the house. No, dad. When I went outside, I saw his truck hadn't returned either, so who said my name?

Perhaps I had just imagined it, as my mind was still a mess from little sleep and losing Jamie. I walked over to the broken window and listened to the wind flowing through a hole in the tape. I pressed it firmly against the fractured surface to seal it.

A sharp pain in my sole dropped me to the floor as blood dripped on the carpet, creating a puddle. The glass in my foot wasn't huge but long and skinny enough to penetrate deeply. I pulled it out and hobbled to the kitchen to grab towels, leaving bloody footprints everywhere. Red liquid seeped through the paper cloth, and I applied more pressure to stop it. The sound of a vehicle pulling into the driveway made me pause.

"Anna, what the hell is this?"

Emma came running into the kitchen, tracking my blood with her. My mother appeared and sighed at the pile of bloody paper towels on her table.

"What happened?"
"I stepped on a glass shard and am bleeding."
"Well, did you have to write on the window with it? It's gross, Anna, and you're going to clean it."
"Window? Mom, I didn't draw on anything."
"Anna, don't argue. Now, let me see your wound. I swear I will be upset if I need to take you to the hospital on a Saturday."

She pulled the towel off my foot, scowled, and left the room. I could hear her complaining to herself from the bathroom and the sound of rifling through drawers. When she reappeared, she had gauze, tape, and ointment.

"Come here."

I sat across from her and put my leg on her lap. She applied cream to the wound, an oversized gauze square, and then taped it several times. Then she walked over to the cupboard under the sink, whipped out cleaner and carpet foam, and set them next to my arm.

"I have to take care of these groceries and feed your sister so you can clean your mess."
"Yes, ma'am."

The window drew my attention when I entered the space. My blood had been used like finger paint to spell my name on the glass in small letters. I eyed my mother in the kitchen, who seemed oblivious. How could she have thought I did this?

I grabbed the cleaner and scrubbed it off before my father came home and saw it. Then, I moved to the floor, applied foam to the carpet, and scrubbed my crimson smears. I glanced back to the window, half expecting my name to have returned like some cruel nightmare, but it didn't.

Morning came faster than I had hoped as I threw the covers back to a bloody mess by my feet. During the few hours I slept, the bandage had come off my wound, staining my pink sheets.

After cleaning and patting my foot dry, I reapplied more ointment and a Band-Aid. Then I went to strip the blankets from my bed and start laundry before heading to the kitchen.

The new window had a nice clear view of the birch tree in our front yard. Its white peeling bark reminded me of the paint around the windows at Jamie's house. He always said he had lead poisoning from it and just laughed it off. I stared out of it now, watching my father take the remnants of the old broken one to the curb.

The sound of Emma's voice came from behind me. Her speaking isn't what scared me; it's what she said when she spoke.

"Jamie," she said, twisting her body at the waist.

"Emma, what did you say?"

"Jamie."

"What about Jamie?"

"He's here."

"Emma, don't say that. Why would you say that?"

"Because," she said, sticking her finger up her nose.

"Emma, he's not here."

"He's there," she insisted, pointing behind me.

I didn't know what I expected when I turned around, but I should have known better. Emma is only two and can't see Jamie because he's deceased. I went into my room and shut the door in her face, but she kept knocking.

"Jamie, Jamie, Jamie," she chanted.
"Shut up, Emma."

Her footsteps thumped away as she fled to tell our mother I was being mean to her. Like I cared. Within moments darkness appeared under the crack in my door. I braced for my mother to come in and yell at me, but the shadow disappeared as fast as it arrived. I flopped back on the bed, let out a sigh of relief, and went to sleep.

My panicked heart raced as I realized I couldn't move. My arms and legs were pinned like a stake in the ground. I couldn't talk because an unforeseen force imprisoned my words.

A visible breath in the air chilled my face as it hovered above me. I gasped as its dark face pulled the breath from my lungs and whispered.

"Annnnnnnnnnaaaa."

My screaming woke up the entire house. The terror held me in place, keeping me from moving. My door whipped open, and my father ran in.

"Anna, what? What's the matter?"
"Something's in here."

"You're having a night terror. Come on. Get up and shake it off."

"No, dad. Something was holding me and saying my name."

"It's just a dream."

"I'm telling you it was real."

"Well, there's no one here," he said, looking at me like I was nuts.

"Not anymore."

My mother stood behind my father, shaking her head. She had to work early, and my screaming wrecked her peaceful night's rest. Emma leaned against her rubbing her eyes, and started to cry. My father rolled his eyes, picked Emma up, and carried her out of the room.

"Mom, I think it's Jamie."

"Anna, don't be silly. You had a nightmare. Now, go to sleep."

Shutting my door behind her, she left me alone, frightened. I slid out of bed and switched on my overhead light. Bracing my hand on my mattress, I peered under the bed, but dust bunnies and old notebooks were all I found. I know it's him. Why is he tormenting me? Am I being punished for causing his death? Could he be trying to tell me something?

I racked my brain for an explanation that made sense as I turned the light off, climbed beneath the blankets, and gazed at my ceiling. Every time I closed my eyes, I could see his handsome baby face. The way he made me feel didn't fade with his demise, as I could sense him now more than ever.

Dismal as it may sound, I wanted it to be him. I needed it to be Jamie. I needed him to tell me who killed him so I could bring them to justice.

Emma dove into bed with me and pulled the covers over her head. I peered under them, smiling at her.

"What are you doing?"
"Hiding," she giggled.
"Can I hide with you?"
"Yes."

I scooted myself beneath the sheets with her, but the sparse space made it difficult to avoid her musty cereal-laden breath. Unable to stand it anymore, I yanked the comforter off us and began tickling her. Her obnoxious giggles made me laugh, and I leaped off the bed to chase her to the kitchen.

My eyes burned from lack of sleep and a brewing headache. The abandoned hallway to the restroom seemed to get longer and longer. The faster I went, the further away it appeared. I guess that's what happens when you hold it too long.

Squeezing my cheeks together as tight as I could, I slammed the toilet lid open just in time. Now I know how my father feels when he rushes in ahead of me. This must be why. I almost didn't make it, and crapping my pants nearly made my list of most embarrassing moments.

The flushing across my face and the anxiousness in my belly told me I needed to find something to occupy my time. The cabinet above the sink creaked as I opened it to remove the stomach medicine. The nasty pink liquid in my throat gagged me like I brushed my tongue too far back.

I swung the door closed, and a dirty hand slapped the glass where my mirrored face stared back at me.

Thrashing wildly, I fell backward, landing in the bathtub. Stars danced in front of my eyes as Jamie's ghost stroked my face before I lost consciousness, and everything turned black.

I woke up in the hospital with my parents sitting next to me. The pounding in my head felt like a jackhammer on a sidewalk. When I sat up, vomit launched from my mouth and splattered on my mother's hand.

"Anna, are you okay?"

"Sorry, mom," I said, wiping puke from my bottom lip.

"It's okay, honey."

"Joe, go get the doctor."

My father left the room, and my mother explained what had happened.

"Anna, you fell and hit your head on the faucet in the tub. They had to shave part of the back of your head to staple it, but don't worry; it will grow back."

"Mom, it's Jamie."

"Anna, stop with this nonsense. You've been through a lot, and you see things."

I opened my mouth to speak when the physician came in. His pen light shined into my sensitive eyes, making me squint as he gave me a quick, impatient rundown of what would come next.

"Anna, you have a head injury. You may experience light sensitivity, dizziness, blurred vision, and headaches. It's going to take time, but these symptoms will dissipate. We will remove the staples in about seven to ten days, but you will be out of school for at least a week. Do you have any questions?"

"No."

"Very well," the doctor said as he patted my knee and left the room.

There are so many other reasons I'd like to miss seven school days, but this wasn't one of them. I couldn't wait to leave the sterile, cold hospital.

We stopped at the local ice cream shop on our way home. My parents bribed Emma with it if she promised to be good. I understood their logic, but sugar is the last thing a hyper-two-year-old needs. I thought about the encounter with Jamie's ghost in the bathroom. He didn't mean to hurt me.

The fall and subsequent head injury were just consequences of trying to get my attention. Now that he has it, I have to find out what he wants from me before he accidentally kills me. My mother did not believe me, and I needed someone to tell everything I could trust to help me figure this out. When we returned home, I called Lisa.

"Can you come over? I want to talk to you about something."

"I'll come by after dinner," Lisa said.

"Okay. See you then."

The pain behind my eyes created a pressure I had never felt before. I grabbed my ice pack, flopped it across my forehead, and laid back on the sofa. Emma's screaming from the kitchen seared through me like a samurai sword.

"Shut up, Emma!"
"Anna, be nice to your sister."

Here I am, the one with head trauma who needs quiet, yet I'm the one who's getting yelled at. Life can be cruel sometimes, but that's how things go.

Chapter Seven-Divulge

Lisa's eyebrows raised unnaturally. Her back-and-forth pacing became annoying as she tried to understand what I was telling her.

"So, what you are telling me is that your now-dead ex, Jamie, is stalking you from beyond the grave? You do realize how crazy you sound, right?"

"Lisa, I know it's hard to believe, but look at me. Everything that has happened started after he died."

"Perhaps he's trying to tell you something or, even worse, punish you for leaving him."

"That's what I'm scared of."

"Someone killed him, so his soul can't rest until they find out who."

"If only I knew. The way things are going, Jamie will end up killing me before he gets his message across."

"Have you tried talking to him when you know he's there?"

"What would I say?"

"Tell me what you want, for starters. You could just cut to the chase and ask him who his killer is."

"What if I'm afraid to know?"

"Do you think it's someone we know?"

"I don't know. I guess I'm just being paranoid."

"I have an idea. My older brother has a friend whose grandmother is a medium. I can see if she would be willing to help you."

"I don't have the cash for that."

"Tell your mom we are going to the movies this weekend, and you need money. Offer extra chores. I'll do the same, and then we should have enough."

"Okay. I'll try," I said skeptically.

"Good. For now, though, let me look at that bald patch on your head."

After Lisa left, I went to my bedroom to lie down. A throbbing headache drove a stake through my temples with unrelenting pain as I curled into a fetal position. The walls closed in around me, and the room became frigid. Clouds of my cold breath surrounded my pale face as the face of Jamie appeared before me.

"Annnnnaaaaa..."

"What? Tell me. What do you want from me? Tell me," I yelled.

The lamp beside me crashed to the ground, shattering into a million pieces. Running feet pounded down the hall, followed by the frantic turning of a locked bedroom door. My body launched out of bed and landed hard on the floor. Jamie took me by my legs and pulled me towards the window.

"Stop! Please, tell me what you want!"
"Yoooooouuuuu…"

Jamie vanished when my father busted through the door like a madman. Blood dripped from my head and elbows from being dragged across the ground.

"Anna, what happened?"

"It's Jamie, dad. He's here!"

"Anna, nobody is here, and he is dead, remember?"

"I know he's dead, dad, but he's here."

"You mean a ghost?"

"Yes. That's what I'm telling you. He tried to pull me out of the window and take me."

"Listen, you have a head injury. You fell asleep, had a nightmare, and tumbled out of bed. We should take you back to the hospital tomorrow."

"I don't want a doctor, dad. I need a medium."

"Anna, I've had a long day at work, and I'm tired, so please, let's just put this to rest for now."

"Where's mom?"

"She will be back soon. Emma had a rash, so your mother took her to urgent care to have it looked at."

The nasal snoring coming from my father carried into the kitchen as I made a glass of hot chocolate, dressed in warm clothing, and sat on the porch steps.

The frosty air awakened my exhausted face and cooled my frightened lungs. A mail truck pulled in front of our house, and the mailman came towards me, holding a package.

"Do you live here?"

"No. I'm just squatting on their porch."

"Funny. Someone handed me this box on the street. I guess I'm a courier now, so here you go."

He turned around to leave, slipped on the step, and fell. I stifled a laugh the best I could, but the way he went down made it hard.

His robust frame rolled off the steps sideways, and landed in a snow drift face first.

When he sat up, his snow-covered face appeared as though someone had hit him with a whipped cream pie. He got up, brushed himself off, and stalked down the sidewalk.

The box addressed to me barely weighed anything. I opened it and glanced inside—a blood-covered knife wrapped in a bloody cloth rest at the bottom.

My hands instinctively threw it away from me. It stained the snow when it landed, and the wind picked up a note that was with it, blowing it across the yard. I chased it down and stomped it with my foot. Picking it up by the corner, I read the bloody message.

'I'm sorry. It was an accident.'

My legs felt like rubber bands as I ran to fetch my father. Still snoring and unconscious, I stood over him and yelled his name.

"Dad."

"Anna, you scared the crap out of…what the hell is that."

"Jamie's killer sent it."

"Anna, set it on the coffee table and go to your room."

"But, dad."

"No. Don't argue. Not this time. Go to your room. I'm calling the police."

I stormed out and headed to my room. Soon the cops will be here, and I'll be asked many questions to which I don't know the answers. Why would the killer send me the knife instead of disposing of it? Were they trying to earn my forgiveness with an explanation of what happened?

I stood in my room, waiting for the cavalry to arrive. A crow perched on the phone lines in front of my house, and I wondered. Was this the mate of the one killed by our unforgiving window?

A marked and unmarked vehicle showed up in front of our house. The detective from the cemetery exited, and so did the patrolman from the other cruiser. The detective spoke with the man in uniform and proceeded down our sidewalk. His eyes shifted

up to my face staring at him through my
window. After giving me a quick nod, he disappeared
inside.

The aggressive quivering in my stomach moved
the contents of my intestines closer to their exit. I
bolted to the bathroom, slamming the door behind
me. My shaking hands barely grasped the toilet paper
as they tingled from the lack of oxygen.

This wasn't my first anxiety attack, so I knew how
to manage it. Just because I was smart and did well in
school didn't mean a difficult test wouldn't throw my
mind and body into turmoil.

The door rattled with insistent knocking, but I
didn't answer. The gagging stench made me bury my
face in a towel, and I wasn't ready to breathe it in
yet. The turning knob of the unlocked door forced my
hand.

"I'm on the toilet," I hollered.

"Anna, the detective needs to speak with you," my
mother said from the other side of the door.

"Well, it's going to be a few minutes. My stomach
is upset."

"Okay. There is medicine in the cabinet."

"I know."

Of course, I knew that. The last time I used it,
Jamie's ghost almost killed me. This time when I
opened the cabinet to take the nasty pink liquid, I
didn't close the door.

The fan did nothing to ease the noxious fumes of
my days-old stomach contents. I washed my hands
and exited the bathroom. My mother stood outside,
waiting for me.

"You, okay?"
"What do you think?"
"I'm sorry, Anna."

She put her arm around my shoulder, brought me to the kitchen, and guided me to my seat.

The detective sat across from me, drumming his fingers on paper. His brown eyes intently set on mine when he began questioning me. I hated when people stared at me, so I shied away from him and focused on something else.

"Anna, who handed you the package?"
"The mailman."
"Did he say who gave it to him?"
"No. He just said someone on the street."
"Okay. This part is important because we will dust the box for fingerprints and check for DNA. Did you touch it or note inside?"
"I only touched the outside of the box, but the note blew away, and I had to step on it. I grabbed it by one corner."
"Do you know which corner?"
"No, I was too busy freaking out, dumbass," I yelled.
"Anna," my mother shrieked.
"Okay, okay. Everyone, calm down. Couple more questions, and then I'm done."
"Do you know who could have sent this?"
"Of course not."
"Anna, I have one last question, and it's going to be hard, but I have to ask it. Did you kill Jamie?"

Before the words finished leaving his mouth, I jumped from the table. The tightening of my fists and pounding heart told me how angry the question made me. The detective could see it, too, so he stood and put both hands up, trying to calm me.

"How dare you. I loved Jamie. I would never hurt him."

"I'm sorry. I know it's a difficult question, but it's one I'm required to ask."

"Well, you have your answer; now go away."

My feet barely felt the floor as I stormed back to my room. How dare he accuse me of something so awful. I glanced out of my window when I heard a door close. The police were leaving, and the detective carried the evidence box to his open trunk. He peered up at me one last time before climbing into his car and driving away.

I am not the killer, but whoever it is, knows me. Their guilt just let me know Jamie died from a knife wound and that it was accidental.

After a restless night's sleep, I asked Lisa to see about making arrangements to meet the medium her older brother's friend knew.

I frantically scrubbed the kitchen counters, vacuumed the carpets, and even cleaned the bathroom to raise enough money to pay for her.

My mother came in and gaped around, confused. Her eyes set on me with suspicion, and I put my head down. She probably assumed my head injury did more damage than initially thought. The last thing I needed was for her to take me to the doctor, so I blurted out my and Lisa's lie.

"Lisa wanted me to see a movie with her and grab lunch. I thought if I did some extra chores, it would help fund it."

"Really? Were you going to ask or assume I would say yes?"

"I'm sorry. I need to get out of the house. Please?"

"Okay. Switch the laundry for me and fold the clothes in the dryer. When you're finished, come see me."

"Thanks, mom."

"You're welcome."

My mother paid me $40, and Lisa's dad gave her even less. At this rate, we need to do some crowdfunding to pay for the reading.

As fate would have it, we ran into Jamie's friend from school while walking around the city, and he agreed to help pay the difference. His eagerness to find Jamie's killer paled compared to mine, but everyone grieves in their way. He gave us the money and told us to let him know if the reading revealed any new clues.

We rushed down the walkway to the medium's place of business. When we entered, a woman pushed passed us in tears and burst through the shop doors. Lisa and I glanced at each other and shrugged. The medium appeared unexpectedly beside me, making me jump.

"You have a dark spirit following you, young lady."

Her right eye, clouded with severe cataracts, threw me off, and I began shaking. Lisa grabbed my hand and gave it a reassuring squeeze.

"Yes. He's hurting me," I said to the medium.
"No child. He's trying to get your attention. Come with me."

She led us down a dank green hallway and into a room with red-painted walls. The low-burning candles on the black cloth-covered table produced only a sparse amount of light. We sat across from her with our palms resting neatly on its surface.
She placed her hand palm side up in front of me and wiggled her fingers, showing her need for payment. I put the money in her hand, and she clenched it tightly, crushing the cash in our grasp.

"You know who hurt him," the woman hissed.

"No. I don't. Let go. You're hurting me."
"He's coming…."
"What? Wait, I want to leave. Please let me go."

Lisa grabbed our intertwined hands, and tried pulling us apart, but her grip was strong for an old lady. The candle between us blew out, and the pitch-black room turned cold.

"He's here," she whispered.
"I'm scared. Let me go."
"Annnnnnaaaaaa…."
"No! Let me go, please."

My frame lifted out of my seat and catapulted into the wall. I pinned myself flat as someone's hands moved from my legs to the front of my abdomen while I screamed. Although I could not see him, I could feel Jamie's body and face inches from mine.

"Annnnnnaaaaaaa…looooook…insssssiiiiide…"
"I don't understand. Look inside what?"
"Theeeee boooook…"
"What book?"
"Heeeeeeeeerrrrrrrrrs,"

Like nails on a chalkboard, his screaming last word left me with more questions than answers. Did he mean that the killer was female? If so, whose book? The medium? Lisa? Someone else?

The room fell quiet, and the candle flickered back to life. Lisa sat on the floor crying, and the older woman, still in her chair, said nothing as an unsettling smile spread across her face. Vomit made its way to my esophagus, and I ran out of the shop to throw up.

When I turned to Lisa, her ashen face told me she believed me. My concerns grew even more now that Jamie had just given me a crucial clue.

I often ask myself, how well do people really know each other? They say not to judge a book by its cover, but what if the cover is just that? A false impression of who you are inside to gain access to someone's world and everything they cherish.

From the outside, Lisa was a sweet and innocent person whom I'd known since kindergarten. Could it be possible that she's a crazed killer?

I eyed her across the cafeteria table. Neither of us ever talked about what happened at the mediums shop. We were both still trying to process it. Lisa stood up from the table.

"Can you watch my bag? I have to go to the ladies' room."

"Sure," I said, smiling.

"Thanks."

As soon as she disappeared around the corner, I unzipped it and leafed through her notebooks. My hand reached for her journal when Lisa appeared in front of me.

"Anna, are you going through my stuff?"

"I was just looking for a pen."

"Really? Because from far away, it looked as though you were checking every textbook."

"I'm sorry. I just had to be sure."

"Be sure of what? That I'm not the killer?"

"Lisa…"

"It wasn't me, Anna. Here. The only thing left to go through is my journal. Take it."

She tossed it across the table at me and walked away. I wouldn't be reading it. It just became clear to me that I had made a mistake. Lisa has always been a great friend, and I betrayed her. My mistrust may have just cost me our friendship.

A popular girl and her friends from the funeral stopped me in the hallway as I exited the cafeteria. I've always hated her and the stuck-up snobs she flanked herself with.

"Well, well, is the dynamic duo having troubles?"

"Leave me alone, Tonya."

"Alone? Isn't that difficult for you? You know, since Jamie's haunting you and all?"

"How did you know that?"

"Come on now, Anna. Do you think your loser boyfriend's ghost is coming for you?"

"I don't want to talk about it."

"Well, that's too bad because we are talking about it. Is that what happened to your head? Did he try to kill you? Maybe, you tried to kill yourself because you feel guilty. Did you kill Jamie? Come on, tell us. Confess."

"I have to get to class."

I tried to walk away from her, but she grabbed my arm. My fist swung through the air, striking Tonya in the center of her face, and breaking her nose. Blood gushed over her lips, and onto her silk blouse as she burst into tears while screaming.

Her friends helped her off the floor, and a teacher brought me to the principal.

I sat and waited for word about Tonya's condition from the nurse. The principal came into her office and pushed the door around. She leaned against the front of the desk with her arms crossed and sighed.

"Anna, would you like to tell me what that was about?"

"She grabbed me, so I hit her."

"Is that the only reason?"

"No. Tonya wouldn't stop talking about Jamie."

"What about him?"

"She asked me if I killed him and tried to kill myself because of it."

"Anna, I know things have been tough for you. Your grades are suffering, and now this. I have no choice but to suspend you for breaking Tonya's nose. Your mother and father will be here soon to pick you up."

"I'm sorry."

"Save your apologies for Tonya. Now, go sit in the lobby and wait for your parents."

"Okay."

My parent's voices came out like an out-of-tune radio. Bits and pieces came through, but most of it sounded like static.

Assaulting Tonya earned me two weeks' grounding, no allowance until Tonya's medical bill was paid in full, and no phone privileges.

Sitting on my bed, I stared at the wall and wondered, could it have been Tonya? She always hated me as much as I hated her. Was it possible that she was his killer? All my conspiracy theories and guesses made my head spin, so I tried to focus on Jamie's message.

Maybe 'the book' he was talking about was a metaphor for someone instead of something. And by 'look inside' meant for me to look inside myself. Does he think I know the answer? I wish he could have just told me. Emma came into my room with a book and sat next to me.

"Anna, here."
"Do you want me to read to you?"

She nodded as she flicked her lips with her fingers. Reading to Emma is something I enjoy, so I made the time even though I still had a pile of homework.

We were about halfway through the story when my room became uncomfortably cold. Emma snuggled up to me, but I had stopped reading, for we were no longer alone.

"Jamie," Emma murmured.

I stared at Emma when his name came out of her yap. Her eyes were fixed on the blank space between two windows in my bedroom.

The book we were reading flew out of my hand and shattered the mirror above my dresser. Emma shrieked, jumped off my bed, and ran out of my room screaming.

"Noooooooo, Annnnnnnnaaaaa."
"Please, stop. What do you want from me?"
"Booooooook…looooooook"
"Whose book, Jamie?"

The window fogged, and three letters appeared one by one.

M-O-M

I dropped to my knees in disbelief right when my mother entered. Glass crunched under her shoes as she walked closer and closer. I moved away from her and towards the once transparent pane that now brandished her name.

"Anna? What is it?"
"Was it you? Did you kill Jamie?"
"What? Are you on drugs? Why would you say such a terrible thing? Where is this coming from, young lady? Who has been filling your head full of these lies?"
"Jamie wrote 'mom' on the window, and when I went to see a medium with Lisa, he told me to find the book. Her book. It's you. You're hiding something. Tell me."

She closed her eyes and let out a sigh of surrender.

"Anna, I'm sorry. Please come with me. We need to talk."

My mother's collection seriously tested the engineering of the bookshelf it sat upon. She is set in her ways and prefers holding a physical book in her hands. I tried to lean her toward digital, but she refused.

On the highest shelf of her bookcase, she pulled a sideways book lying on top of the others and gave it to me.

"Anna, I only kept this from you for your protection. I didn't read it, as it's not my business. But if it helps you move past this, I guess it's worth it."

She left me standing alone in her room. I sat down on the bed and opened the book. An envelope fell onto my lap, then slid to the floor. I picked it up and stared at it. Inside was a folded handwritten note from Jamie, dated the day before he died.

Anna,

You are my everything. I've never met anyone like you, and I know you feel the same. I love you. I'm writing this letter to make sure you know how I feel if something happens to me. The atmosphere around me has changed since you left me. I have a strange emptiness that I can't seem to shake. It's like I'm already dead, but I don't know it yet. Please call me Anna. I need you in my life to be whole again.

Love,

Jamie

He somehow sensed his eminent death, which may be why he's haunting me now. I wasn't there to save him.

Salty tears dropped onto his last words, blurring them permanently. The lump in my throat gagged me, and the uncontrollable cough that followed took my breath away.

The hardwood bit into my knees when I struck the floor. Completely engulfed in pain and heartache, my body failed me.

"Anna, breathe. Look at me," my mother said, joining me on the floor.

Even though my mother's eyes were level with mine, I couldn't see her. The room darkened around me, and stars seemed to come from outside to serenade me as I passed out.

I now understood why my mother held the letter from me. She thought ahead of time like moves on a chess board.

As it turned out, she had made the right choice. The note tipped me over like a sacrificial pawn, landing me right back in a medical facility. Its black and white checkered floor tiles were no different from the game itself.

All I wanted to do was go home, but the doctor decided to put me on a temporary psychiatric hold until I could speak to a psychiatrist in the morning.

They took my shoelaces from my sneakers, and I only had a cushion to sleep on. No blankets, no sheets, and no sharp objects were allowed in my room. An orderly came and checked on me every hour.

As I lay on an uncomfortable sponge meant for dishes in my naked isolation room, I thought about Jamie's letter.

How did my mom even get it? Did he give it to her, or was it mailed? He would have sent the note via carrier pigeon if he had one.

Speaking to the psychiatrist about everything that happened since Jamie's demise was the hardest thing I had ever done. She didn't judge me, however. She set her pen and notepad down, removed her glasses, and rubbed her temples.

"You don't believe me, do you?"

"Anna, it is not my job to believe or not to believe. My job is to help you find a way to cope with your grief and provide you with the tools necessary to get well."

"Which are?"

"Counseling for one. Jamie's death is not your fault, yet I can tell you feel you are to blame. In addition, anti-anxiety medications could be beneficial for you to take on an as-needed basis for sudden attacks. Finally, I need you to start a journal."

"You mean to write my feelings down and stuff?"

"Not just your feelings. Questions you want to be answered, phrases that make you happy, your dreams, and your nightmares."

"And my encounters with Jamie's ghost?"

"Definitely. If you see Jamie and he's speaking to you, you must write down what he says when he says it. Otherwise, the message may not be remembered correctly. The mind can be very tricky in the face of fear. Do you understand?"

"I think so."

"Good. Now, come here and pick a journal."

The sizeable metal desk drawer screeched open, and a vast assortment of journals filled the interior. Some were just a solid color, but quite a few had images on them. One of them had an old muscle car sitting in front of a beautiful sunset by the mountains.

Jamie loved muscle cars. He would get so excited when one passed us on the street. His eyes would light up like a child on their first amusement park trip, and he would tell me that he's 'going to have me one of those someday.'

I gazed at it for so long that I became lost in my mind's blank space. The psychiatrist had to touch my arm to bring me back.

"Anna, are you okay?"

"Yes. I'll take this one."

"Okay. Well, we are done here. Your mom is outside in the lobby waiting for you. I can't tell her anything we discussed in your session as it's confidential, so she may barrage you with questions. Don't feel obligated to answer. Your thoughts are your own, and what we discuss stays in this room."

"Okay."

"It was very nice meeting you, Anna."

"You too."

I don't know whether the doctor spoke to my mother or didn't know what to say, but she didn't ask me anything. Not a single word came from her the entire ride home. The tension in the air made me feel claustrophobic, and I couldn't wait to escape the enclosed space.

When we pulled up in front of our house, the detective stood on our porch with my father.

I hesitated before getting out of the car, and I'm happy I did. The detective walked towards us, nodded at me, and climbed into the cruiser parked in front of us.

I let out a sigh that sounded like a balloon being let go without being tied as my father came to the car and opened the door.

"Hey, kiddo."
"Everything okay, dad?"
"Yeah. He's just asking some follow-up questions, is all."
"Oh."
"Hungry?"
"Not really," I sighed.
"Okay. I guess you can watch us eat then."
"Honestly, I'm tired, so I'm going to lie down."
"I understand. You had a long night. We can talk later."

My mother stopped before my father and placed her forehead against his chest. He kissed the top of her head and pulled her into him. Now I feel worse.

Everything that was happening with me was taking its toll on them, and I didn't know what to do about it. I removed a pen from my desk drawer, sat on my bed with my new journal, and wrote my five Ws.

Who killed Jamie?

What more does Jamie want from me?

When is my life going to be normal again?

Where did mom get the letter?

Why did this happen?

I closed the notebook and set it on my nightstand. Tomorrow, I will get the answer to at least one of my questions.

Chapter Twelve-Deceit

Last night, I slept. I don't know whether it had something to do with writing down my questions and worries or I was just that tired.

Things have been quiet, which concerns me. I feel like I'm in the eye of a storm that could turn violent at any moment.

Asking my mother about the letter will be uncomfortable, but I needed to know. It had to be important, or Jamie wouldn't have gone out of his way to get it to me. The sound of running water brought me to the kitchen.

"Morning, Anna."
"Mom, how did you get Jamie's letter?"

The question stopped her from doing the dishes, and she turned to me.

"Does it matter?" She turned her back to me and went back to scrubbing.
"It does to me."
"Your father."
"Dad? Where did he get it?"
"Anna, I don't know. Why don't you ask him?"
"I'm asking you."
"And I've answered. Now, eat your breakfast."

Her angry tone forced me to clam up. The loud clanking sound of plates stuffed into the dishwasher made me leave the kitchen. She was done talking, and I didn't have the nerve to challenge her further. After I got dressed for school, I stopped in Emma's room. She was holding her favorite teddy bear and a picture book beside her bed. I shuffled the hair on her head and told her I would see her later.

When I left the house to go to school, I nearly walked into Lisa.

"Hi."

"Hey, Anna."

"Look, Lisa, I'm sorry about the other day. This whole thing has me going crazy."

"So, I've heard."

"Don't tell me everyone at school knows."

"No, just me. I only know because I called looking for you after I heard you punched Tonya. Your mom told me you were in the hospital. Is everything okay?"

"I had a severe anxiety attack. Jamie had written me a note the day before he died, and it set it off."

"A note? Where did it come from?"

"She said my dad gave it to her."

"Where did he get it?"

"I don't know, but I'm going to ask him after school."

"I'm sorry we fought."

"Me too."

An excessive number of eyes glared at me as I made my way to my locker. I unlocked it to put my things inside, and the notes fell out. Apparently, I have a fan club, and Tonya had more enemies than we thought.

At lunchtime, our typically abandoned table became filled with new faces. Some people wanted to know what she said to make me react the way I did, and others wanted to know what it felt like. Their questions were undeserving of an answer from me.

Where were all these people before now? Do they think they can swoop in, and I'll open my life to them like some talk show host? My life is not some form of entertainment, and neither is Jamie's death. It didn't stop them from prying it out of me, so I made a public announcement from the top of the cafeteria table.

"Listen up, everyone. If you want to know why I hit Tonya, ask her yourself. If you want to know how it felt, keep pissing me off, and I'll show you personally."

The assistant principal came over to the table and ordered me down. I found myself back in the principal's office once again. I didn't get suspended or detention this time. This time she just counseled me on conveying my feelings properly.

She handed me a pass for my next class and advised me that she would have to suspend me if it happened again.

My message has worked. Everyone avoided coming near me the rest of the day or ignored my presence.

Lisa met me outside my last class so we could walk home. She had been bombarded with people trying to get her to answer their questions.

"I'm sorry, Lisa."

"It's okay. I told them to quit bugging me, or you'd punch them next."

"You're so funny."

"So, are you going to ask your father about the letter?"

"Yes."

"Call me and let me know who gave it to him or where he got it from."

"I will."

We parted ways, and I headed to my house. My father met me on the porch.

"Hey, dad."

"Hey, kiddo. How was school today?"

"It was all right. Dad, where did the letter come from?"

I blurted the question out. His face twisted to the side as if the question confused him.

"What letter?"

"The one from Jamie."

"Oh. Jamie's uncle gave it to me. I didn't want you to be more upset than you were about everything, so I had your mother put it up."

"When did he give it to you?"

"Anna, I don't remember. Does it matter?"

"I guess not."

"Your mom made spaghetti. Let's go eat."

We sat around the table and ate in silence. Spaghetti is usually my favorite meal, but I didn't have much of an appetite. My stomach felt unsettled.

I stared over at Emma and began laughing. Soon my mother and father joined in breaking the dull icy air. Emma had a large noodle across her forehead, and her entire face resembled a sauce pie.

She giggled excessively at our laughter at first, then stopped. Picking up a meatball from her tray, she launched it over the table and hit my father in the face. Most of the time, this would create more laughter, but not this time. What she said when it struck him made us stop laughing too.

"Liar."
"Emma, don't throw food at your father."

Emma grabbed another meatball and threw another one at him.

"Liar," Emma screamed.

My mother snagged her hands to stop her, but they stopped launching the meatballs.

"Liar, liar, liar," she chanted.

Finally, my mother ripped the tray off her highchair and took her to the bathroom. I glanced at my father, who wouldn't look at me.

"Dad, what is she talking about?"
"Anna, your sister is two. I don't know what goes through her mind from day to day."
"Whatever," I said, rolling my eyes.

I threw my plate, spaghetti, and all in the sink, then stormed off to my room. Emma may only be two, but something inside me believed her, and I wanted to know what he was lying about. I grabbed my journal and wrote another question, along with a note.

What is dad lying about?
Go to Jamie's uncle and ask him about the letter…

After sulking in my room for hours, my mother came to see me. She sat down on the bed and put her hand on my leg.

"Anna, your sister kept saying 'liar' because your father and I were arguing earlier."

"About what?"

"I made a mistake, sweetheart."

"What do you mean, mistake?"

"I slept with someone else. I don't know how your father found out, but he did, so we argued. We talked it out, and everything is fine now. I did a terrible thing, and I was wrong. I'm sorry."

"Mom, who was it?"

"It doesn't matter now because it's over. I broke it off."

"How could you do that to dad?"

"I told you. It was a mistake."

"Fine. Whatever. Can I be alone now?"

"Of course."

Sleep eluded me for hours. My mind worked hard to figure out whom my mother cheated on my father with. What a bomb she had dropped on my complicated life. What she did could have affected us all, but my father forgave her, and I wondered why.

They've been together for almost twenty years. I guess that would be a lot of wasted time if they were to call it quits now and try starting over.

As I read, my weary eyes began to blur, so I tried again to fall asleep. This time it worked.

The sound of the smoke alarm and loud banging woke me. My father burst into my room with my mother and Emma screaming.

"Fire. Get out now."

We ran through the house and out the back door. Our barely clothed bodies shivered on the snowy sidewalk as our home burned.

Thankfully, our neighbors came out and offered us shelter. The fire department and police arrived in minutes, but nothing could have saved it. The wind and bitter cold made it much more difficult to fight. The water kept freezing in the hoses, and the wind took the water that did make it through in every direction but the house.

"Dad, what happened?"

"I don't know, kiddo. I guess we will know more when they investigate."

"Where are we going to go?" I asked.

"We can go to the old house; then we will see," my father grimaced.

"We don't have any clothes there."

"Anna, we can get some tomorrow. Let's be thankful that we all made it out alive tonight."

Here we go again, back up the winding mountain of doom. The house creeped me out, and I hoped we wouldn't have to return after the last time.

It is bad enough that Jamie is haunting me; now we have no choice but to stay at the haunted house. My father drove up the treacherous road defensively, but in the end, our vehicle found a ditch a quarter mile shy of the place.

"Son of a …."

"Dad, are we stuck?"

"Yes, Anna."

"Listen, you girls stay in the car, and I'm going to hike to the house. I'll get a fire started and turn on the lights. I'm going to check for blankets and bring them back so we can walk in. There is no sense calling anyone tonight in this storm. No one would make it through."

He climbed out into the knee-deep snow and stumbled out of the ditch. I peered down at the slippers the neighbors gave me to walk in. My feet would feel the bite of frost by the time I reached the house.

I looked at my mother's face and the worry she carried. Emma had fallen asleep on her shoulder, oblivious to the current crisis.

"Mom, are you okay?"

"No, Anna, I'm not."

"We have insurance on the house, right?"

"Yes. We are covered for fire."

"Good. One less thing to worry about," I said, trying to be optimistic.

"Just one?"

"Mom, is something else going on?"

"Anna, not now. Let's focus on getting to the house without freezing to death, shall we?"

A flashlight flickered back and forth toward us. My father's silhouette was barely visible through the blustery white curtain. He had a shovel in one hand and an armful of blankets in the other. Before opening the door, he shook the excessive snow off the covers and placed them on the dashboard in front of the heat.

"I'm going to start a path while those covers warm up. Give me a few minutes, and I'll come back to get you."

He closed the door and disappeared behind a snowy wall. The sound of a scraping shovel moved in rhythm as my father picked up and threw the white crystals.

My mother grabbed the blankets on the dash and felt them for warmth. She shook one out and threw it in the back for me.

"Anna, once your father opens that door, you listen to what he says. Stay on the path. If you aren't careful, you can get lost in this and freeze to death."

"I'll be careful."

"Good. Now, here he comes. Are you ready?"

"Ready as ever."

My dad pulled the door open and put his hand out to my mother. He wrapped the blanket around them both and turned to me.

"Anna, stay right behind me. Please hang on to my jacket. Right here. Do you see this loop? Grab it; no matter what, don't let it go."
"Okay."

The raging air whistled through my body and blew the blanket up behind me like a cape. Although I tried to remain on the path, the wind blew me sideways, and I stumbled into the deep embankment. My slipper got buried beneath the wet mound of marshmallow fluff, but I couldn't release my father's loop, so I pressed on.
The frozen ground beneath my bare sole nipped at the unprotected skin, but it wasn't long before it disappeared.
Thankfully, the house's light led us through the thick drifts. As the snow stung her face, Emma's cries rang through the howling wind like a dying animal.
With my only focus being on the hoop on my father's jacket, we reached the house faster than expected and not a moment too soon. Once inside, my mother berated me.

"Anna, where is your slipper?"
"I lost it."
"Come here and sit down by the fireplace. I need to soak that foot," she said as she left the room.

She returned moments later and placed my numb appendage into warm water. Emma began crying, and she abandoned me to tend to her. My father grabbed a few more logs and set them on the fire.

"You okay, kiddo?"
"My foot is dead, but I'm doing great."
"Don't be dramatic. Everything is going to be fine."
"When?"

He didn't respond. I turned my attention to the fire and thought about our house. Everything we own burned to the ground. This dilapidated hell hole is all that is left besides our car, that's parked in the ditch.

Embers from the fireplace floated up and out of sight as they exited the chimney with the smoke. My life is in that burning flame. Its raging heat turns everything we own into glowing ember dust and carries it away, never to be seen again.

The tension in the air felt like the high pressure that comes with an impending storm. I saw my parents speaking with each other down the long dark hallway. My father caught me watching and backed my mother into a nearby room for privacy.

Emma slept peacefully on the couch as I soaked my lifeless foot in water. The wind whispered through the cracks in the windows and vibrated their panes as cracking wood made my nervous eyes look to the ceiling.

A telling sign of how the house felt about the weather; I worried it might fall upon us as we sat inside its unsteady shelter. My parent's fight escalated behind closed doors as the muffled voices became clearer.

A door slammed, followed by the sound of my mother screaming. I jumped up and ran towards her shrieks. The nerve endings in my foot either had returned or the adrenaline had kicked in, aiding my advance.

The door opened for me when I reached it. My mother's body was pressed against the wall with her hands on her face. Her eyes led me to what held her there like a statue. Blood dripped from the sharp edges of the broken glass, and snow blew inside from its now open center.

"Mom, where's dad?"

She said nothing, so I made my way cautiously to the jagged void where the window once stood. My father lay unconscious on the ground outside in a mound of snow. The letters spelled out the same message on his bare chest as before.

L-I-A-R

I pulled on his boots that still sat by the door, grabbed a blanket, and threw the front door open.
Greeted with a face full of white shards, I fought through the blinding, deep snow to help him.

"Dad! Get up."
"Anna, I'm sorry."
"Don't be sorry; get up. You need to get inside, or you'll freeze. Now, come on."

I put his arm around mine and headed back to the house. Once we entered the living space, I glimpsed at the couch where Emma once slept.
Its empty status sent a shockwave of panic through me. I dropped my father onto the sofa and searched the room.

"Emma…? Where are you? Now is not the time for hide and seek."

Her giggles echoed through the house, but I couldn't see her. My father made no motion to help me look. Instead, his eyes fixed on the fire as he accepted his fate-whatever that may be.

"Mom is Emma with you."

"Anna, don't come in here."

Her voice from the room came out shaky and petrified. I caught a glimpse of Emma at the opposite end of the hallway. Her pointer finger came out of her mouth and moved me in her direction as she ran away again.

"Emma," I said, running after her.

Her giggles brought me to the kitchen table, where she sat in front of a letter. The familiar cigarette burns made me think its message was meant for me, but then I started to read.

Joyce,

My heart skipped when you said you would leave him for me. No one will stand in the way of our love. I could never see myself without you. You are my soul mate, and I am madly in love with you. Let's not put this off any longer. Come away with me, and let's have our happily ever after.

Love,

Adam

Burn holes were present throughout the message, and the word 'liar' is scattered across multiple locations on its surface.

I picked it up and stared at it in utter disbelief. The letter is for my mother, from Jamie's uncle. Things were becoming uncomfortably clear as I walked out of the room to find her.

I found her and my father sitting together on the chaise. Emma had followed me in and sat on the chair by the fire with a bag of chips, waiting for the show to begin.

"What the hell is this?"

"Anna, I'm so sorry. I made a mistake."

"A mistake? You cheated on dad with Jamie's uncle and called it a mistake?"

"Anna, your mother, and I have talked it out. We are going to go to counseling and work on our marriage. I know you are upset, but…."

"Upset? I'm furious. Mom, you are the biggest hypocrite and liar I've ever seen. I can't believe this. You forced me to break up with Jamie because you said he was bad news and would affect my future, but that was a lie. All this has happened so that you could keep and cover up your affair with his uncle."

"Anna, I'm sorry."

"How long? How long were you cheating on dad with him before Jamie and I met?"

"Six months."

"Wow. Do you know what you've done? He would still be alive if it weren't for you. We would still be together, and he would still be here."

"Anna, that is enough. I said I'm sorry, and your father and I are working it out. Jamie is gone, and we can do nothing to change that now."

The bucket of water my foot had been sitting in tumbled into the fire with such force that it bounced back out. Cold filled the air, and whispering words chilled the dark, silent space.

"Liaaaaaaaaaar…"

I looked from the plastic container by my ankles to my parents. There is more to the story than what she is telling me, and Jamie wants me to know.

"Who's the liar, Jamie? Show me."

The bucket sailed through the air and struck my mother in the legs. My father held her around the waist to steady her uncontrollable shaking. I moved before her and grabbed both arms.

"Tell me. Jamie won't stop until you tell the truth."
"There's nothing to tell Anna. What do you want me to say?"
"Liaaaaaaarrrr….,"

The word howled through the house, and the front door flew open, crashing against the wall. Emma pounced up and down in her seat, chanting Jamie's name over and over again.

"Jamie, Jamie, Jamie…"

Emma fell silent, staring at something behind me, and my parents did the same. The widening of their eyes and ashen faces told me they could see it too.

I could feel a presence there, but fear didn't come over me. It gave me the strength and will to continue my forceful interrogation.

"Mom, tell me what happened."
"Honey, I don't know what you're talking about."

The chandelier in the dining room swooped down from the ceiling and crashed to the ground. Pieces of glass cast a wide-reaching path resembling crystal ice across the hardwood in our direction.

"Liaaaaaarrrrrrr…!"

The bellowing repeated word brought a gust of icy wind, knocking us over.

My father stepped away from my mother and joined sides with me. He, too, knew there was something more than just her infidelity.

"Joyce? If you're keeping something from us, you need to tell us, or Jamie will tear this house apart or worse."
"Joe, I don't…."

Before the words left her mouth, an apparition of darkness came behind her and yanked her feet out from under her. My father chased my mother's screaming, flailing body towards the back door and out of sight. Emma came to me, put her hand in mine, and pulled me down the dark walkway.

Emma's insistence led my heavy legs down the long hall in the direction our mother was dragged. Fear didn't grip me or Emma like it should have, as my father desperately tried to keep our mother from being drug into the dismal basement, and failed.

The door slammed itself shut, locking them inside its dungeon's depths.

A voice came from behind us and startled me. When I turned around, Jamie's uncle, Adam, had ahold of Emma, and she began crying.

"What are you doing?"

"Where is she?"

"Who?"

"Your mother," he hollered.

"Basement. Put my sister down."

"Not until I speak to your mother."

I stepped aside to give him access to the secured door. Pounding thumped on the other side, followed by cries for help.

"Anna, open the door. Where is the key?"

"Well, Adam, why don't you ask your nephew?"

"What the hell are you talking about?"

My eyes fixed on the kitchen window behind him. When he turned around, letters formed one by one.

Adam lowered Emma to the tile, and she ran to me.

"What the hell?"
"Adam, what happened to Jamie?"
"I don't know what you're talking about."

I took Emma by the shoulder and backed us away from him. His face twisted with confusion, followed by sudden surprise when a shadowy apparition appeared before him, lifting him off the tiled floor. I wondered what went through his mind as he sailed across the room and struck the wall on the other side.

"Adam, the only thing that will save you is the truth."
"Anna, what is happening?" He asked, looking frantic.

The basement door clicked and cracked open. Now unlocked, my parents had an opportunity to escape.
When my mother saw Adam, she ran to him, and so did my father, but for different reasons. He grabbed Adam from the floor and shook him violently while my mother hollered for him to stop.

"What did you do? Did you burn our house down? Was it you? Did you come here to finish the job? Why are you here? Answer me," my father screamed in his face.

Adam took one look at my mother's injured face and saw red. He fought against my father, and a violent brawl ensued. Fist after fist flew back and forth while blood cast through the air staining the walls with new red paint.

My mother grabbed Emma and pulled her out of harm's way, but I didn't react in time. One of Adam's swings missed my father and struck me hard on the head, instantly taking my hearing to one side.

A loud screech followed by a malevolent force threw the men away from me and out of the kitchen door. They landed just outside the house in a pillow-soft snowbank. My father and I locked eyes right before the door slammed shut, locking them out.

The dark presence appeared as I lay on the tiled floor. I could feel but not see Jamie's hand on my face. My mother tried to come to me, but he shrieked at her like an insidious creature, making her back away.

Tears fell like torrential rain from my face as Jamie somehow showed me the truth with his transparent touch. My father and Adam had come back in through the open front door and made their way down the hall.

"Tell me what happened, mom. I know you killed him. Just tell me."

"I'm sorry, Anna. It was an accident. He saw me with Adam, and he threatened to tell you. I chased after him and tried to reason with him, but he wouldn't listen. I didn't want your father to find out, so I tried to scare him with a knife. We struggled, and I slipped. The knife went into him when we fell to the ground. I didn't mean to kill him. Please forgive me."

"Forgive you. He's dead because you wanted to cover up your affair. I will never forgive you."

My father didn't know that my mother had been involved in Jamie's death. I could see in his shocked face. It is one thing to cheat on him, but another to murder someone to hide it. He picked up Emma, walked towards the living room, and out of sight.

Adam slid his back down the wall and landed on the floor next to my mother.

His hand covered hers and held it while she cried. Their mutual deception had taken Jamie's life and ruined ours. I could feel Jamie's presence still with me and knew there had to be more.

"Adam, did you know?"

"Yes."

"Did you help her cover it up?"

"Yes."

"Did you light our house on fire?"

"I'm sorry. I just wanted your mother back."

"Get up, both of you."

"Anna, what are you doing?"

"Mom, get off your ass and do what I say," I hollered.

My screaming demanded their immediate compliance and attention. Once on their feet, I nodded for them to go inside the cellar.

"Anna, please don't do this. This could destroy all of us if it gets out. Please…"

"Get down there, now!"

Mom and Adam descended the stairs until they reached the bottom. The door shut and locked on its own as the sounds of sirens blaring closed in on us in the distance. I walked outside and stood next to my father and Emma.

The storm slowly dissipated, and the shining sun peeked through the clouds, illuminating our exhausted bodies. A new day began as my haunting nightmare ended.

The police questioned my father and me separately, then had us sit in one of the patrol cars until the detective working Jamie's case arrived.

We waited for my mother and Adam to be led out of the old house, side by side, in matching handcuffs. The detective walked over and asked us to join him in his car. As he explained to my father what happened next, I glanced up at a moving curtain in the attic window of our house.

The dark figure slowly transformed into Jamie. His baby face and brown eyes smiled at me, then disappeared behind the sheer.

His murder has been solved, and he has no reason to stay anymore, but I hoped he would. The detective explained to my father that Adam had set the fire.

He saw my father sleeping on the couch, broke the glass, and threw a Molotov cocktail inside. It overshot my father and landed on the rug, igniting it.

My parents were fighting about this in the bedroom before my father was tossed out of the window at our dilapidated home.

He was confronting her about Adam, and she tried to deny that she was still seeing him.

As it turns out, she did leave him, but they had talked about reconciling. She feared my father would create a problem for her, so Adam decided to get rid of him, unbeknown to my mother. Adam also confessed to helping my mother cover Jamie's accidental death.

No one mentioned what occurred inside the house about the paranormal activity. Despite multiple attempts by locals and authorities to gain more insight into the occurrences leading up to them being called, no one said a word. Who would believe it anyway? Besides, the house would never sell if anyone knew what happened there.

Charged with involuntary manslaughter and facing up to twenty years in prison, my mother took a plea deal. My father sobbed to himself as the bailiff led my mother away to begin her ten-year jail sentence.

Neither of us wasted the energy it would take to look at her, despite her pleas for forgiveness.

Because he had never committed a violent crime, they ran Adam's sentencing concurrently. Despite being charged with attempted murder, arson, and covering up Jamie's murder for my mother, he only received fifteen years.

It seemed like a far cry from what he deserved, but I wasn't a prosecutor or a judge, so what did I know?

Lisa held my hand as we drove away from the courthouse. My rock through this traumatizing ordeal; I couldn't ask for a better friend. She leaned forward in her seat and whispered something into my father's ear. He nodded and changed the direction of the car.

We arrived at the cemetery where Jamie was buried a few minutes later. My father dropped Lisa and me off and told us he would return soon.

"Thank you, Lisa."
"You're welcome."

Passing several tombstones and statues, we trekked our way up the hill to Jamie's grave. Dead flowers surrounded his headstone, and Lisa helped me clear them away.

She stepped away to give me the privacy and opportunity to say goodbye. As I lay down on the still soft mound of dirt piled high on Jamie's casket, I could sense his presence beside me. I squeezed the earth between my fingers and cried as I spoke.

"It's over, baby. You can rest now. I'm so sorry this happened to you. I will always love you and hope to see you again someday. Rest in peace, my love."

A shadow cast over me, and I thought it may have been him, but it wasn't. My father stood next to Lisa with a bouquet of white roses and handed them to me.

Their soft, perfect petals stood for the once youthful innocence of Jamie's life, now a pillow on top of his final resting place. The thorns of the roses were a harsh reminder that even something so beautiful can cause pain if you're not careful.

Grief had consumed me for so long that I felt guilty for letting it go when it subsided.

Finding Jamie's killer should have lifted a great weight off my shoulders, but that would never be the case.

My father divorced my mother shortly after her conviction and decided to move us out of state. The publicity of the case, too much to bear any longer, pushed us away from the quiet town where we had been born and raised.

With only a month left of high school and no one knowing my history, making new friends came easily.

Lisa and I spoke every day. We talked about being accepted into the same college and looking forward to reuniting in the fall, but that isn't all. I told her about my concerns over my father's recent behavior, and she told me to intervene as it sounded like he could be depressed.

Despite Emma's repeated attempts for attention, my father stopped caring about his appearance and paid little to no attention to her. She would finally give up and sit quietly in front of the television. This broke my heart, and I grew tired of seeing it happen.

"Dad, get up!"

"Anna, I'm tired. Just leave me be."

"You're depressed and need to see someone."

"No, I'm not."

"Yes, you are. We need you, and even though you are sitting in that chair, you're not here."

"Anna, what do you want from me?"

"I want you to be present. We need you. I want you to be our father, and if you don't think you're capable of the task, then maybe I should call Aunt Barbara."

"Leave my sister out of this."

"Then get off your butt and do your job!"

"I'm sorry, Anna."

"Listen, dad, I know you're upset, I am too, but I'm not going to let it affect the rest of my life or those around me. I've made peace with what's happened, and so should you."

"Make peace with it! Your mother is a killer! A cheater and liar who's in prison. How can I make peace with that."

"Wow, dad. Did you forget she killed someone I loved? Sitting around moping and ignoring your responsibilities is not going to change anything about the situation. It's just going to push us away from you. You already lost mom. Are you trying to lose us too?"

"Of course not!"

"Then get help! Seek counseling, call a friend, talk to me or someone you trust before it's too late."

He put his head in his hands and began sobbing. Emma ran over and gave him a huge hug. He pulled her in his arms and held her. I came to them and joined in their embrace. He stroked our heads and cried until his tears ran dry.

"I'm so sorry, girls. I promise I will do better."

After a few weeks of counseling, my father started to come out of his depression. He enthusiastically spoke to neighbors about my upcoming graduation and how happy he was that I was accepted into Yale.

He signed Emma up for gymnastics to help her expel some of her crazy energy.

One day before my graduation, my father invited me to watch Emma learn gymnastics. She had only come to a few classes, but she loved it. I didn't know until I arrived the reasoning behind my sudden invitation. My father talked with the woman sitting to his left for most of the class. It would appear he met a divorced mother, Laura, whose daughter is in the same class as Emma.

The chemistry they shared was undeniable, and I not only approved but also went as far as inviting her to ice cream after the girl's class.

As her daughter, Lexi, and Emma, talked, I realized their instant friendship reminded me of Lisa and me when we were that age.

The girls wanted to play on a nearby playground, so I volunteered to take them so Laura and my father could have privacy. While I took turns pushing the girls on the swing sets, my father interacted with Laura. They were already in love and didn't know yet, but I did.

How they stared into each other's eyes mimicked how Jamie and I had looked at each other the first time we met. The connection happened instantly and was sealed with a very public first kiss resulting in both sides blushing.

My father turned and glanced at me. I gave him an approving nod and continued to swing the girls. He is going to be okay, and so am I.

The End

DEDICATION

This book is dedicated to all the girls and boys that believe they have found their first love. If someone objects, make the decision yourself whether to leave or to stay. If you let someone decide for you, you may regret it for the rest of your life.

Special thanks to Angela Johnson of Endless Thoughts Publishing for your help with editing.

In memory of Mary Updike, who always welcomed everyone as if they were family. We love and miss you.

Sidero – Book One

The Carpenter's Chameleon – Book Two of the Sidero series.

www.ingramcontent.com/pod-product-compliance
Lightning Source LLC
Chambersburg PA
CBHW060506300726

48975CB00008B/2666